KITTEN KINGDOM

～Tabby's First Quest～

Tabby's First Quest

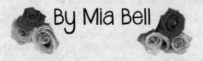 By Mia Bell

Scholastic Inc.

All rights reserved. Published by Scholastic Inc., *Publishers since 1920*, 557 Broadway, New York, NY 10012, by arrangement with Working Partners Limited. Series created by Working Partners Limited, London. SCHOLASTIC and associated logos are trademarks and/or registered trademarks of Scholastic Inc. KITTEN KINGDOM is a trademark of Working Partners Limited.

The publisher does not have any control over and does not assume any responsibility for author or third-party websites or their content.

This book is a work of fiction. Names, characters, places, and incidents are either the product of the author's imagination or are used fictitiously, and any resemblance to actual persons, living or dead, business establishments, events, or locales is entirely coincidental.

ISBN 978-1-338-29234-3

10 9 8 7 6 5 4 3 2   19 20 21 22 23

Printed in the U.S.A.   40
First printing 2019
Book design by Baily Crawford

With special thanks to Conrad Mason

Table of Contents

Chapter 1

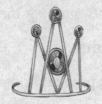

ROYAL KITTENS

Princess Tabby peeked out from behind an empty suit of armor. She moved her ears up and down to signal to her brothers. *All clear!* Then she ran into the hallway.

Her purple-and-gold skirts swished as her paws sank into the thick red carpet. She ran past old paintings of catkings and catqueens, her brothers scrambling behind her. Tabby's whiskers shook with excitement. *This beats studying the royal family tree again!* she thought.

"We did it!" squealed her younger brother, Leo. He rolled into a somersault and sprang up again, his big yellow eyes shining with excitement.

"Careful!" said Felix, their older brother. His tail twitched nervously beneath his purple jacket. "If we're caught sneaking candy again, we'll—"

But before he could finish, Leo tripped over his own sword. The little orange cat landed flat on his face, and a rainbow of catnip candies burst out of his pockets.

They scattered everywhere. Tabby saw one go rolling toward a huge golden door . . .

"The Great Hall!" gasped Felix. "Mom and Dad are in there *right now*!"

Tabby's heart raced. She ran after the candy as fast as her paws would carry her. *Thump!* She pounced on the candy, trapping it in her front paws.

"That was close," sighed Felix. "We should get back upstairs before Nanny Mittens wakes up and sees we're not at our desks."

But Tabby couldn't resist looking around the edge of the door. The Great Hall was huge, big enough to play a furball match in. Long red-silk banners hung on the walls.

Each one was decorated with the golden claws of Mewtopia.

At the far end of the hall, Tabby's parents sat on a stage in their golden thrones. Bright morning sunlight shone down through a big cat-shaped window.

A group of finely dressed lords and ladies stood around the stage. They purred in praise as Tabby's father, King Pouncalot, read to them from a paper scroll.

"Greetings, kitizens of Mewtopia!" he said. His deep voice echoed through the hall. "I declare the first law—that King Pouncalot and Queen Elizapet are the rulers of the land! The second law is that the royal family will always protect Mewtopia from danger . . ."

"Oh my whiskers!" said Leo, leaning past Tabby. "I thought the Golden Scroll Ceremony wasn't until tonight!"

"They're just practicing with a paper scroll, silly," Tabby told him. "Weren't you listening at morning milk time? When Mom and Dad read the laws tonight, the last sunbeam of the day will shine through that window. It will fall onto the Golden Scroll."

"Then everything Mom and Dad say will magically appear on the scroll," added Felix. "And those are the laws everyone has to obey."

Just then, a royal guard turned their way.

"Quick!" Felix ran off in a flash of black fur.

Tabby grabbed Leo and hurried after her older brother. The three royal kittens ran until they reached the big spiral staircase that led up to their chambers. Tabby sighed. She had enjoyed their short adventure almost as much as Leo had. But now it was over, and she didn't want to go back to their boring quarters.

In the stories she read, the brave kitty heroes never had to study history books or practice bowing and curtsying all day. They were too busy going on adventures.

One day I'll have an adventure of my own, she thought. *Just like in the stories.*

"I wish we could have a look at the *real* Golden Scroll," said Leo sadly.

Tabby's ears popped up. "Why don't we?" she said. "Nanny Mittens will probably still be sleeping."

Prince Felix bit his claws. "I don't know, Tabby. Sneaking candy is one thing. But breaking into the royal treasure chamber . . ."

"Last one there's a wimpy mouse!" shouted Leo, and he dashed off down a dark hallway.

Are we really doing it? wondered Tabby. She

felt scared . . . but excited, too. She grinned at Felix. "We don't want to be mice, do we? Let's go!"

A few moments later, they stood outside the heavy door of the treasure chamber. The hallway was dark and silent. There were cobwebs in every corner.

"I'm not sure about this," Felix whispered. But Leo reached up and pushed the door open with a creak.

"*Wow!*" said all three kittens at once.

Inside were piles and piles of glittering treasure, lit by torches blazing on the walls. Tabby didn't know where to look first. There were jeweled crowns, sparkling diamond necklaces, gold-framed mir-rors . . . *Some of them are probably even magical!* she thought.

"Leaping fleas!" she said, pointing to a marble stand in the middle of the cham-ber. "There it is!" On top of the stand sat a small glinting object. It was thin and gold, wrapped around a wooden rod, and tied with a thick red ribbon.

The Golden Scroll!

Leo ran over, followed by Tabby and Felix. Together, they untied the ribbon, then opened the scroll. The gold surface was blank but so shiny that the three kittens could see their faces reflected as if it were a mirror.

Tabby sighed happily. "Just think! One day we'll use the scroll to make our own laws."

"Ooh, I bet we'll come up with really good ones!" said Leo. "Like . . . cream instead of bathwater. In fact, no baths at all!"

"How about extra tuna for kittens whenever they want?" said Felix, smiling.

"Agreed!" said Tabby. "And royal kittens should be allowed to go on adventures!" *As long as they're not too scary, anyway,* she thought to herself.

BANG! The door burst open. The kittens jumped.

Someone stepped into the treasure chamber. He was tall and bent over, wearing a black cloak with a hood covering his face.

The torchlight flickered. Leo's mouth fell open, and Felix's ears bobbed up. Tabby could feel the fur rising along her back.

Then she thought of all the brave kitty heroes in her books. *They wouldn't be scared of a hooded stranger!*

She took a deep breath and stepped forward. "Who are you?" she asked.

The figure came closer. His shadow fell over the royal kittens. Then he bowed low.

"Greetings, Your Highnesses," he said. His voice squeaked in an odd way. Tabby couldn't see his face, but two yellow eyes stared out from under the hood. "If you'll excuse me, I have come to collect the Golden Scroll for polishing."

Tabby tugged on her whiskers. "That's

odd," she said. "Normally it's the royal gold-smith who comes to polish the treasure."

The stranger smiled. "Well, I'm afraid he's a bit tied up today." He reached into his cloak and drew out an envelope. "This letter from the goldsmith will tell you all you need to know." He tossed it, and it spun through the air.

Felix caught the letter in both paws. On the back of the envelope was a blob of golden wax, pressed with a tiny paw print.

"That's the seal of the goldsmith, all right," Felix said.

"What clever kitties you are," said the stranger. "Please, read it."

Tabby tore open the envelope.

Dear fluffy kitty friends,
Please give the Golden Scroll to this nice
cat . . . OR ELSE!
Hugs and snuggles,
The Royal Goldsmith

Tabby took the Golden Scroll from Leo. "I think we should check with Mom and Dad," she said.

"Check if you must," snapped the stranger. "But the ceremony is only a few hours away. If the scroll is not polished by then, the magic won't work."

"I don't like the sound of that!" said Felix. He began to bite his claws again. "It would ruin the whole ceremony."

Leo nodded. "We'd better give it to him."

"All right," said Tabby reluctantly. But as she handed the scroll to the messenger, she saw something odd. His paws weren't furry like most cats. Instead, they were pink.

The messenger slipped out of the room, a thin pink tail swishing behind him.

Leo gasped. "Did you see that?" he said, pointing. "His tail was all long and scaly! Not a single hair on it."

"And his paws were pink, too!" said Tabby. "What do you think it means?"

"Maybe he's one of those hairless cats," said Felix. "Like the Great Wizard Sebastian." Then he looked at a silver grandfather clock standing in a corner and jumped. "Oh my whiskers! Nanny Mittens has been catnapping for ages. We'd better get back to our room before she wakes up!"

As the three royal kittens raced back up the stairs, Tabby couldn't stop thinking about the strange messenger. There was something very familiar about him. *I feel like I've seen him before*, she thought. *But where?*

Chapter 2

JUST A STORY

"Trout twisters!" cried Leo as he emptied his pockets onto the blanket. "My favorite!"

Tabby's brothers sat in Leo's big comfy basket, stuffing their faces with sticky tuna chews and sour lemon sardines. Nanny Mittens was still snoozing on her cushion in their study chamber across the hall. The kittens' rooms were up in the highest tower of the palace, the safest place they could be.

But Tabby didn't feel hungry. In fact, there was an odd, sinking feeling in her stomach. She lay in her own basket, staring into space. *Those pink paws didn't look like they belonged to a cat*, she thought. *In fact, they didn't even look like paws!*

"Something's not right," she said at last.

"I know," groaned Leo, holding his tummy. "I think I ate too many twisters!"

"I meant with that messenger!" said Tabby. "Do you think—"

But before she could finish, a loud snort came from the study chamber.

"Nanny Mittens is waking up!" whispered Felix. "Quick, we have to hide the candy!"

Felix and Leo each grabbed a corner of the blanket. They tipped the candy onto the floor. Then Tabby swept it behind Leo's basket with her tail. *Just in time!*

Nanny Mittens came through the door, smoothing down her apron. "Bless my whiskers, I fell asleep!" said the big white cat. "I do like a nice catnap, I tell you. Now, where were we?"

"You were about to give us our mid-morning milk, Nanny," said Leo hopefully.

Nanny Mittens chuckled. "Silly Leo!" She stroked his ears. "We already had our milk, remember? I think that's what sent me to sleep in the first place. Now it's time for a lesson. Come along, kitties."

Tabby tried to forget about the strange messenger as she and her brothers followed Nanny Mittens to the study chamber. It was a little room with a blackboard. Maps of Mewtopia hung on the walls next to shelves full of old leather-bound books.

Tabby, Felix, and Leo sat at the three wooden desks while Nanny Mittens began to write on the blackboard. "Today we are going to learn about Queen Gwenda the Fourth," said Nanny Mittens. "She was your great-great-great-grandmother. We'll start with the thirty-nine laws she made. Law number one . . ."

Leo buried his head in his paws. *I don't blame him!* thought Tabby. They had already spent half the morning learning King Lionel's twenty-eight laws.

She stuck a paw in the air. "Please, Nanny Mittens," she said. "Couldn't we learn about something fun?"

Nanny Mittens frowned. "Fun? What's more fun than rules?"

"Anything!" whispered Leo, but luckily, Nanny Mittens didn't hear him.

Nanny Mittens stroked her whiskers thoughtfully. "We could learn about the correct way for a royal kitten to wave to kitizens," she suggested. "Or how to cut a ribbon with the special golden scissors."

"What about a story?" asked Leo, sitting up suddenly. "I bet Queen Gwenda had some adventures before she started making laws!"

"Don't be silly, Leo!" hissed Felix.

But Nanny Mittens nodded. "You're quite right, my little fluffball. Queen Gwenda was a very naughty little kitten when she was young. But surely you don't want to hear about that?"

"Oh yes we do!" cried Tabby. "Please, Nanny Mittens, tell us a story!"

"Pleeease!" added Leo.

Nanny Mittens smiled. "Well, maybe a short one."

As the big white cat shuffled over to the shelves, Tabby grinned at her brothers, and they grinned back. She knew that every time Nanny Mittens read them a story, she ended up asleep.

Nanny Mittens chose a thick old book and settled into her favorite rocking chair. "Gather around, kitties!"

The royal kittens sat on the floor. Nanny Mittens blew dust off the book. Then she opened it. *"Once upon a time . . ."* she began. *"There was . . ."* Yawn. *". . . a young kitty princess whose name was . . ."* Yawn. *". . . name was . . ."*

Her head fell, her eyes closed, and she began to snore loudly.

"Yes!" said Leo, punching the air. "No more lessons today!"

The book slipped from Nanny's paws. Tabby caught it just before it hit the floor.

Felix took a blanket from behind the rocking chair and gently laid it over Nanny's lap.

Tabby opened the book. On the first page, she saw a picture of a young kitten sword fighting with lots of different enemies. The scariest was a big brown rat with yellow eyes. Tabby blinked. *He reminds me of the messenger in the treasure chamber . . .* she thought.

"What's wrong, Tabby?" asked Felix. "You look like you've seen a bathtub!"

"What if that messenger wasn't a cat at all?" said Tabby. "What if he was . . . a *rat*?"

"What do you mean?" asked Leo.

Tabby dropped the book and ran back

into their bedroom. Her brothers followed. Tabby went to her own bookshelf and ran a paw over the old leather books. *A Prince among Mice . . . Tales of Silverpaw . . . Adventures of the Cat Burglar . . .* "Here!" she said, pulling out a dusty book even older than the others. Wiping the cover, she read the title out loud. "*The Legend of the Wicked King Gorgonzola.*"

Felix's ears stood up in surprise.

Leo bounced around the room. "Will you read it, Tabby?"

Tabby opened the book. At once, she saw a picture of a rat. He had shiny dark fur, yellow eyes, and—

She gasped.

"That scaly tail!" said Leo.

"And those pink paws!" said Felix.

"I knew I recognized him," said Tabby. Her tummy filled with butterflies. "It's him! The messenger!"

"Who is he really, then?" asked Leo.

"His name is Gorgonzola," said Tabby. She began to read from the book. *"Long ago, rats lived in peace in the underground kingdom of Rottingham. But then the wicked Gorgonzola became their king!"*

Now Leo gasped.

"Gorgonzola was so greedy that he wanted to make Mewtopia part of Rottingham!"

"That's just a story for little kitties," Felix said. But his green eyes were wide.

"That doesn't mean it's not true," said Tabby. "What if we really *have* given the Golden Scroll to the rat king? What if Mewtopia is in danger?"

"Mom and Dad will be so mad at us!" said Leo, his whiskers drooping.

"Only if we tell them," said Tabby.

"But we have to," said Felix. "Don't we?"

Tabby felt a shudder of fear run down her tail, but she ignored it. *I bet a great hero like Silverpaw never went to his mom and dad when he was in trouble!* she thought.

"There's only one thing we can do," she said. She shut the book with a thud. "We'll have to find out for ourselves what's going on."

"You mean . . . leave the palace?" asked Felix.

The royal kittens often sneaked out of their bedroom, but they'd never been outside the palace without their guards.

Tabby nodded. "We gave the scroll away, so we have to make sure it's safe."

"Count me in!" said Leo, looking much happier.

"Well . . . I guess I should come, too," said Felix.

"Hooray!" said Tabby, doing her best to sound brave. She had always wanted to go on a real adventure, but now she had never felt so nervous.

Leo darted over to their old dress-up box

and threw open the lid. "Let's wear disguises so no one will recognize us!"

"Great idea, Leo," agreed Tabby.

"Shh!" Felix cast a nervous glance at the door, his whiskers shaking.

Across the hall, Tabby could just see the furry white shape of Nanny Mittens through the open door. She was moving in her rocking chair . . .

Then she began to snore again. Her apron gently rose and fell.

"Phew!" Felix grabbed a plain shirt from the box and nodded. "Come on, then," he said. "For Mewtopia."

The royal kittens quietly dug through the dress-up box. In a few moments, they looked just like ordinary kittens in plain dresses, shirts, and pants. Then Tabby looked at the swords hanging on the wall.

"We'd better take those, too," she whispered. *I just hope we don't have to use them!*

They took the swords and put on hooded cloaks to hide their weapons.

Then Tabby took some long woolly scarves from the box. She wrapped one around her face, leaving only her eyes showing, and passed one to each of her brothers. Pulling out another pawful of scarves, she began tying them together.

"What are those for?" asked Leo.

"You'll see!" said Tabby. "I've got an idea . . ."

A few minutes later, she had made a rope out of the scarves. She opened the window, threw out one end of the rope, and tied the other to the window frame. "There!" she said. "Now no one will see us sneaking out. We'll climb down and go straight to the goldsmith's shop. If everything's all right, we'll be home in no time."

Felix looked worried. "And what if everything's not all right?"

Tabby took a deep breath. "Then it'll be up to us to get the Golden Scroll back from the wicked rat king!"

Chapter 3

A REAL ADVENTURE

Tabby climbed out the window, holding on tight to the rope of scarves. Outside, it was a warm day, and the palace wall was bright white in the sunshine. She looked at the ground, and butterflies danced in her tummy.

"It's a long way down," said Felix, leaning out the window. His ears stood up with worry.

"Then we'd better not fall!" said Tabby as cheerfully as she could. "Come on!"

Leo climbed out after Tabby, followed by Felix. They pressed their back paws against the wall and lowered themselves slowly, holding on to the rope.

Just keep going, Tabby told herself. *One paw at a—*

"Argh!" The cry came from above. Looking up, Tabby saw Felix's back legs shoot out from under him. He let go of the rope and fell . . .

Quick as a flash, Tabby stuck her tail out. "Catch!" she yelled. As Felix dropped past, he managed to grab hold of Tabby's tail and cling on. He swung below her.

The rope creaked and swayed, but held strong. *That was close!* she thought.

They waited for a moment to see if the noise had woken Nanny Mittens. But she didn't appear at the window.

"Oh my whiskers!" said Felix. "I'd better take the stairs next time. Thanks, Tabby."

Tabby felt her chest puff with pride. *Maybe I can be like one of the heroes in my books, after all!*

A few minutes later, they were standing on the grass at the foot of the wall, smoothing down their disguises. The palace was on top of a hill, and the valleys below were crowded with pretty, colorful houses with sloped roofs, built around a village green. Tabby could just make out little kittens racing around it, playing a game of furball.

Leo flicked his tail happily. "I can't believe it. We're out of the palace! No guards, no royal staff, no one to tell us what to do . . . This is so exciting!"

"No time for excitement," said Felix. "We have a quest!"

The three royal kittens ran across the grass, hopped over a rosebush, and crept into the village. Around them, they heard flutes being played, kittens calling out to friends, and neighbors laughing and chatting with one another. *It's so much more fun out here than in the castle*, Tabby thought. The kittens followed the noises through an alley full of grooming parlors until they came out onto a wide street.

"The Royal Avenue!" said Tabby.

Young kitties ran here and there waving red-and-gold flags. More flags hung on strings above, stretching across the avenue. The royal kittens made their way through the crowds, taking in the sights and sounds. Treat sellers called out cheerfully to one another. They carried trays of rainbow trout-pops and cotton catnip.

Of course, realized Tabby. *Everyone's getting excited about the Golden Scroll Ceremony tonight!*

They passed a fountain of milk bubbling on a street corner. Cats stopped to sharpen their claws on the rough surface of the lamp-posts. The air was filled with the delicious smell of fish sticks, making Tabby's mouth water. It felt strange to be in disguise, with no guards and no one paying them any attention.

"Get your flags here!" called a salescat from a nearby stall. "Flags for the Golden Scroll Ceremony!"

"Ooh, I can't wait!" whispered Leo. "And just think of the fireworks afterward! *Whhhssssh . . . BANG! BOOM!*"

"First we have to find that scroll,

remember?" said Felix. "Or the ceremony won't happen at all!"

Leo's ears flattened. "So how do we find the goldsmith?"

"I think it's this way," said Tabby. She remembered passing the shop while in a royal parade with their parents.

Sure enough, they hadn't gone much farther when Leo called out. "I see it!" He pointed to a tall blue shop at the end of the street. Painted above the door was a huge golden paw print, just like the one on the goldsmith's letter.

As they got closer, Tabby saw a large sign covering almost the whole window.

WE'RE CLOSED TODAY,
SO GO AWAY!

Tabby's heart sank.

"What do we do now?" Leo asked. "The goldsmith isn't here!"

"Wait," said Felix. "Do you hear that?"

The kittens listened closely. Then Tabby heard a mewing sound from inside.

She hurried to the window and peeked around the edges of the sign. "Uh-oh," she said.

The shop was in total chaos. Chairs were smashed, paintings were ripped down, and golden objects were scattered across the floor. *I've never seen such a mess!* thought Tabby.

Then she saw something else. In the corner sat a scared little brown-and-black dappled kitten. She was tied to a chair with thick ropes, and a gag was wrapped around her mouth.

Chapter 4

GOLD DUST

The kitten mewed again from behind the gag.

Tabby pushed open the door and leaped inside, followed by Felix and Leo. The royal kittens ripped at the thick ropes with their claws until the frightened kitten was free. She pulled off her gag and shook her whiskers with relief. "Phew! You saved me!"

Tabby filled with pride. That made two

kitties she had rescued already! She was really doing it. She was being a hero, just like Silverpaw!

The kitten wore a rough brown shirt and had a patch of white fur around one eye.

"Hey, you're Clawdia!" said Leo. "I've seen you at the palace before. You're the royal goldsmith's daughter."

Clawdia's fur stood on end as she stared at them. "Who are you?"

Tabby quickly pulled her scarf down. Leo and Felix did the same.

Clawdia's eyes grew wide. "Meowza— you're the royal kittens! But what are you doing out of the palace? And why are you wearing normal clothes?"

"It's a long story," said Tabby. "Are you all right? What happened?"

Clawdia's whiskers drooped, and she hung her head. "My dad went to visit a friend in Tailwell today, and he left me in charge," she explained. "I was a little nervous. But I didn't think it would go *this* badly."

"This can't be your fault," said Felix, throwing a paw out at the mess.

Clawdia shook her head. "Oh, no—it was a wicked thief who did this! He came in wearing a long black cloak with a hood, and he smashed everything and tied me up . . . Then he took my father's special paw-print stamp! But the strangest part was his tail . . ."

"Was it pink and scaly?" asked Tabby.

Clawdia gasped. "How did you know?"

"That sounds exactly like the messenger who came to the palace," said Tabby. "He must have used the seal on that letter. Then he pretended it was from the gold-smith. But it was a fake!"

"Now he's got the Golden Scroll," added Felix. He began biting his claws again.

And he might just be the evil King Gorgonzola, thought Tabby. "Can you remember any-thing else about him?" she asked Clawdia.

The little cat's nose wrinkled as she thought. "He had very short whiskers," she said at last. "I could only just see them poking out from his hood. And he had a long nose and clawed feet and . . . Ooh! I remember!" She sprang up from her chair. "Something fell out of his pocket. There it is, by the window!"

Leo ran over and picked it up. It was soft and yellow and full of holes. Leo sniffed and then handed it to his sister. "Smells like . . ."

"Cheese!" said Felix. "And you know who loves cheese most of all . . ."

The royal kittens looked anxiously at one another. Tabby knew they were all thinking the same thing: *rats!*

"So it's true," she said. "King Gorgonzola *is* real. And we have to stop him!"

The others nodded.

"Maybe he left some more clues," said Felix thoughtfully. "Let's have a look."

The kittens began to search the shop. Leo peeked inside a golden suit of armor, which had fallen on its side. Felix hopped onto the counter and hunted through piles of gold coins. Clawdia picked up a pawful of pocket watches.

Tabby looked at the floor where Felix

had found the cheese. Then she gasped. "I think I've found something!" she cried. The others quickly gathered around and saw that the ground was sprinkled with something sparkly.

"It's just dust!" said Leo.

"Yes," said Tabby, pointing. "But it's in the shape of a claw!"

"Looks like a print," said Felix. "A *rat's* print! Good work, Tabby. King Gorgonzola must have come from somewhere very dusty."

Clawdia knelt down. "Do you see how red it is?"

"And there are tiny bits of gold in there!"

Felix said. "But what kind of place would have red dust *and* gold on the ground?"

They all fell silent, thinking. But Tabby couldn't think of anywhere. She wished they had spent less time with Nanny Mittens studying old rules and more time studying geography.

Then Clawdia grinned. "I've got it! The gold mine! Dad's always going down there, and he comes back with dusty red paws."

"Let's go right now!" yelled Leo, hopping up and down and swishing his tail. "I'm going to teach that mean rat a lesson!"

Tabby felt excitement bubbling in her tummy. But a little shiver of fear ran through her as well, right to the tip of her tail. *What if King Gorgonzola is waiting for us down there in the dark . . . ?*

She shook off the thought and smiled bravely. "Do you know the way there, Clawdia?"

The little kitten nodded.

Tabby took a deep breath and pulled her scarf back up to cover her face. "Come on, then," she said. "What are we waiting for?"

Chapter 5

FEAR OF THE DARK

Clawdia led the royal kittens into a little lane behind the goldsmith's house. They crept on tip-paw to a larger street. Clawdia seemed to know just where she was going.

As the cobbled path sloped down the hillside, Tabby felt another shudder of excitement. *Soon we'll be outside the town*, she thought. *The farthest we've ever been from the royal palace!*

Sure enough, they squeezed between two houses and came out into a rocky meadow. Felix gasped and pointed at something on the ground. "Another rat print!"

There on a rock was a second sparkling, dusty print. It looked just like the one in the goldsmith's shop.

"Now we know we're on the right track," said Leo. He drew his sword and slashed it through the air. "Game's up, Gorgonzola! Just wait till I get my paws on you, you scoundrel!"

"Hey, watch where you're poking that!" said Felix, pushing down Leo's blade.

Clawdia and the royal kittens hurried across the meadow, which was covered with little yellow flowers. Tabby's chest pounded as the wind blew through her fur, and her paws carried her through the long grasses. *We're having an adventure,* she told herself. *A real one! There's no need to be afraid . . .*

Clawdia stopped at the bottom of the meadow beside a heap of big gray rocks. The rocks were piled around a gateway made of wooden logs. And through the

gateway was a dark tunnel that led straight into the hillside.

Suddenly, Tabby felt the butterflies return to her tummy. *Come on, Tabby! A real hero wouldn't be scared of a little darkness,* she thought. But she didn't feel like a hero anymore. This was very different from reading one of her storybooks, safe in the palace.

"This is the gold mine," said Clawdia. Tabby saw that her fur was all puffed up, and her eyes were huge. "But I've never been inside without Dad before. What if we run into that horrible rat again?" She looked down at the ground. "I'm sorry, but I don't think I can go in there . . . I'm too scared!"

Me too, thought Tabby. But she didn't want to say it out loud. "Don't worry, Clawdia," she said instead. "I'll stay here with you. If Gorgonzola shows up, he'll have me to deal with!" *And that way, I won't have to go into the mine, either!*

"Well, I'm going in!" said Leo. He rushed through the gateway and ran off into the tunnel.

Felix gulped. "I suppose I'll have to go with him, then."

"Wait!" said Tabby. She took off her scarf and quickly unraveled it with a claw, until it was just a pile of wool. "Here, take one end," she said. "If you get into trouble, just pull on it and we'll come after you."

Felix nodded. He tied one end of the string around his wrist and the other around a nearby tree. Then he puffed out his whiskers and hurried off, his tail waving nervously.

A moment later, the darkness had swallowed him, too.

The sun shone down. Tabby and Clawdia waited ... and waited. Tabby couldn't see inside, and she couldn't hear anything except the swaying of grass in the wind. But the woolen thread kept unwinding. *They must be going deeper into the mine.*

The longer they waited, the worse Tabby felt. *Finally, a real adventure ... and I was too scared to go on it!* She wasn't nearly as brave as she'd thought she was, after all. She sighed, her whiskers drooping with sadness.

"Thank you for staying with me," said Clawdia. "I feel silly for being so scared. But I can't help thinking about that mean old rat!" She shuddered.

Tabby curled her tail around Clawdia's. "To tell you the truth, I'm frightened, too. *And* I feel silly. I've always wanted an adventure, and now look at me! What kind of kitty hero is frightened of the dark?"

Clawdia's ears perked up a little. "Well, at least we can be scared together!" Then she gasped. "Did you see that?"

Tabby spun around. *Oh my whiskers!* The woolen thread was jerking to and fro.

"They must be in trouble!" said Tabby.

All her fur stood on end. But this time she knew she didn't have a choice. *Dark or no dark, my brothers are down there ... and King Gorgonzola might be, too!* She took a deep breath. Then she put a paw on her sword handle and stood up tall, trying to feel as brave as possible. "They need my help, Clawdia," she said. "I'm going in!"

Clawdia's eyes grew even wider. Then she puffed up her chest, too, and nodded. "Not without me, you're not!" she said.

The two kitties smiled nervously at each

other. Then, side by side, they crept into the darkness of the mine.

The ground was rocky and bumpy. Following the string of wool, they tip-pawed down a steep slope. Tabby had to hold on to the wall with one paw to keep from slipping. She could only just see Clawdia's yellow eyes shining beside her.

Then she saw something *else* shining. "Gold!" she whispered. Here and there, patches of metal glittered among the rocks.

She was just about to look closer when she saw a light flicker up ahead. She grabbed Clawdia's shoulders and pushed her down into a crouch. "Shh!" hissed Tabby.

Two cats turned a corner, each holding a lantern. They wore sturdy miners' clothes, with pickaxes resting on their shoulders. They disappeared down another tunnel without noticing the kittens. Then Tabby spotted something in the gloom beyond. She climbed over the rocks to a small wooden cart. Its metal wheels rested on a train track. Next to it lay the broken end of the length of wool.

"Oh no!" Clawdia put her paws to her mouth. "How will we know where Felix and Leo are now?"

Worry jittered inside Tabby like salmon

leaping upstream. *Think, Tabby!* She pointed at the cart. "Clawdia, what's this for?"

"It's to move gold around the mine," said Clawdia.

"I bet Felix and Leo went off in one of these carts," said Tabby. Leo wouldn't have been able to resist a ride. "If we get into this one, we'll catch up with them!"

"If you say so," said Clawdia doubtfully.

"Only one way to find out," said Tabby.

They climbed in, and Tabby used her sword to push them off. The cart creaked and squeaked as it rumbled along the track, slowly at first. Then it began to roll faster . . . and faster . . .

"I don't like this," muttered Clawdia.

I'm not sure I like it, either, thought Tabby. And she was about to say so when—*whooosh!*—the cart dived deep into the darkness.

Chapter 6

WELCOME TO ROTTINGHAM

"Whooooooaaa!" yelled Tabby and Clawdia.

They raced downhill, bouncing and bobbing with every curve of the track. Tabby dug her claws into the wooden sides of the cart. Her heart was thumping with fear. *Or is it excitement?* she wondered. She felt Clawdia's paws holding her tightly.

The cart swung around a bend and shot out into a huge cave.

Tabby and Clawdia both gasped. *This place must be ten times bigger than the Great Hall!* Candles glowed in the distance, like stars in the night sky. Tabby saw that they shone from lanterns held by miners. The cats hung from the rocky ceiling on wooden platforms, chipping at gold in the cavern walls. She could hear the clicking and clattering of tools echoing all around. Some of the miners were singing cheerful songs to keep them company while they worked.

"Look out!" called Clawdia.

The track ran along a narrow bridge right through the cavern, with a steep drop on each side. But up ahead, it forked. The track on the right led to a ledge where a group of miners sat eating sardine sandwiches. The track on the left sloped down into deeper darkness.

They had almost reached the fork. *We can't let those miners spot us*, thought Tabby. *They'll make us leave the cave.* She leaned out of the cart and pulled a lever next to the track. At once, they switched onto the darker path.

"No!" yelped Clawdia.

Too late, Tabby saw a red board beside the track ahead, with big black letters painted on it: DANGER!

The cart shot right past the board. Tabby

heard voices yelling from behind. But her eyes were fixed on the track ahead. The rails came to a sudden end, and beyond, there was nothing but a drop.

Meowza!

Tabby felt the cart dip at the front. Then down they fell, still clinging to the side of the cart.

Tabby's stomach leaped into her mouth. The walls of the cave rushed past. Looking up, she saw the ceiling grow farther and farther away. She closed her eyes and held on tight to Clawdia . . .

THUMP!

The cart bounced off a rock. It thunked into another, then tipped on its side. Tabby went flying, head over tail. She landed in a heap with Clawdia on top of her.

Tabby blinked. She wiggled her paws one by one. She opened her eyes and saw the rocky ground they had fallen on. She could hardly believe it. *We're okay!*

Holding on to each other, the two kittens rose to their paws.

"Where are we?" whispered Clawdia.

It was even darker down here, cold and silent except for an echoing drip of water somewhere in the distance.

As her eyes got used to the dark, Tabby saw something beyond the fallen cart. A gap in the rocks, just big enough for them to squeeze through. It was black as night.

Next to it was a wooden sign, half-rotten. Three words were painted on it.

"*Welcome to Rottingham,*" read Tabby. A cold shiver ran through her. They were in Gorgonzola's kingdom!

"That must be where your brothers went," said Clawdia. Her voice shook.

Tabby nodded. *There's no turning back now.* "Let's go," she said.

She crept into the dark passageway, holding on tightly to her sword. Stone steps led down into another cave, even bigger than the one above. This cave was full of huge rocks, little streams, and pools of still water. Fires burned here and there, and rats gathered around them to keep warm.

In the very middle of the cave stood a shadowy castle built out of rough gray rocks. *It looks just like the royal palace*, thought Tabby. Except it was old and crumbling, as though no one was looking after it. And instead of the red-and-gold flags of Mewtopia, black banners hung from the towers. On each one, there was a picture of a piece of crumbly cheese speckled with blue. It wasn't just any cheese . . . it was the worst and stinkiest of them all: *Gorgonzola*.

A path ran from the bottom of the steps to the castle gates. Tabby and Clawdia tip-pawed down and ran along it. Once, a rat looked up, and they had to duck behind rocks. But at last they reached the castle.

The big wooden door was unlocked, and they hurried inside.

"Yuck, it stinks of cheese in here!" said Clawdia, wrinkling her nose.

Tabby looked around the gloomy hall. There were lots more old wooden doors. *But which one should we go through?* Then her ears pricked up. "Did you hear that?" she whispered.

Both kittens froze as they listened. Someone was talking in a strange, squeaky voice. *A familiar voice* . . . "That's him!" hissed Tabby. "The messenger who came for the scroll."

"The rat who tied me up," said Clawdia.

"King Gorgonzola!" they said together.

They dashed across a faded old carpet, following the sound of his voice. They ran through an archway at the end of the hall, then down a long hallway. His voice was getting louder and louder.

"I think he's in there!" said Clawdia, pointing to a door that stood half-open.

Holding her breath, Tabby crept over and peeked around the door.

The room beyond looked like the Great Hall back home in the palace, but the walls were crumbling and everything was covered in dust. And the figure on the throne was nothing like King Pouncalot or Queen

Elizapet. *Leaping fleas*, thought Tabby, *it really is him!*

King Gorgonzola looked even scarier than the picture in Tabby's storybook. His fur was shiny with grease, Gorgonzola's yellow eyes sparkled, and one ear was torn. But worst of all was his horrible smile full of teeth that were crooked and rotten. Tabby shuddered.

"The thirty-first law," said King Gorgonzola grandly, "is that all trout twisters will be replaced with Parmesan pops! The thirty-second law is that all the kitty homes will be turned into a giant trash dump! The thirty-third law is that

Mewtopia will be *crushed* and all cats will become servants of Rottingham!"

"What's he doing?" whispered Clawdia.

"I think he's inventing new laws," said Tabby. "And if he has the Golden Scroll, he can make them come true! He just has to read them out loud at the ceremony tonight, when the last sunbeam shines through the window." *He's going to make himself king of the cats as well as the rats, just like he wanted to do in the storybook . . . and destroy Mewtopia!*

"Please, Your Rottenness," said a little voice. "Please, may we have a tiny scrap of cheese?"

Tabby saw three smaller rats kneeling in

front of Gorgonzola's throne. They looked very thin.

"Don't be silly!" roared Gorgonzola. "Why should I share my lovely smelly cheese with *you* filthy rodents?"

"Of course, Your Stinkyness," said another rat. "It's just . . . we *did* capture those kitty princes for you . . ."

Tabby's breath caught in her throat. *Are my brothers all right?*

"Perhaps we could have some as a reward?" said the third rat. "If it please Your Revoltingness?"

"No rewards!" screamed King Gorgonzola. "Not until I'm king of Rottingham *and*

Mewtopia, too! Speaking of which, I must be off now for the palace."

The rats hung their heads.

Tabby had never felt so scared, but she had to do something. *Here it goes...* She drew her sword with a wave.

"There are too many of them!" said Clawdia nervously.

"Didn't you hear?" said Tabby. "They said they captured my brothers!"

But just as she was about to charge into the hall, she heard a cry from somewhere deep in the castle. "Help! Help us!"

Tabby almost dropped her sword. She would have known that voice anywhere. *Felix!*

"Help! Please!"

And that's Leo!

"Come on," cried Tabby. She grabbed Clawdia and ran back down the hall. "It sounds like they're in trouble!"

Chapter 7

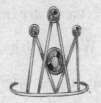

JUST LIKE SILVERPAW

No time to lose! Tabby pounded across the stone floor, dragging Clawdia after her.

"Help!" called Felix again. Tabby came to a halt. She listened hard.

"I think it came from that staircase," said Clawdia, pointing.

Tabby nodded, and they ran down the stone steps. Torch flames flickered as they hurried by, heading deeper into the darkness beneath King Gorgonzola's castle. *What if there are more rats?* wondered Tabby. *What if it's a trap? What if King Gorgonzola comes after us?* But she pushed away her doubts and ran faster.

The steps led into a little cave full of shiny cobwebs. Someone had built a fire on the rocky ground, and in its orange glow, Tabby saw, on the far side of the cave . . .

"Felix!" she cried. "Leo!"

Her brothers looked up, eyes shining in the firelight. They were sitting in a metal cage that was barely big enough to hold them, their front paws tied with rope. When they saw Tabby, they leaped up. She ran across and hugged them through the bars, purring in spite of the danger. *They're alive!*

"You came to rescue us!" said Leo when they broke apart. He flicked Felix with his tail. "I *said* she would!"

"Tabby, hurry! The key's over there," said Felix, pointing upward.

Turning, Tabby saw a bit of metal shining way up on the cave wall: a key hanging from an iron peg. Her eyes began to fill with tears. "It's too high to reach," she said.

"Not if you climb on my shoulders!" said Clawdia. "Here, I'll give you a paw up."

Tabby was just about to climb onto Clawdia's back, when she heard footsteps on the stairs.

"Oh my whiskers, someone's coming!" hissed Felix. "Hide!"

Tabby crouched behind the biggest boulder, pulling Clawdia down with her.

Peeking out from her hiding place, Tabby saw three figures step into the cave. *The rats from Gorgonzola's throne room!* But they looked even sadder now.

"I'm so hungry I could eat a horse!" groaned one, rubbing his tummy.

"*You're* hungry, Chedd?" growled another. "I haven't eaten in days. Not so much as a cracker!"

"Pipe down, Mozz," said the third. "I can't even remember what cheese looks like."

They all sat around the fire. "A little

string cheese would taste pretty good about now, eh, Brie?" said Chedd sadly.

The rat called Brie peered over at Felix and Leo and gave a nasty grin. "Maybe we should toast some royal kitties instead," she said.

Leo stuck his tongue out. "Try it and you'll be toast!"

"Bet they taste horrible, anyway," said Mozz with a shrug. "All fishy and hairy! Let's wait until His Disgustingness becomes king. Then we'll have a pile of cheese as big as this castle . . . each!"

"That rat will never be king!" shouted Leo. He shot to his paws, tripped on Felix's tail, and fell against the cage bars.

The rats squealed with laughter as Felix helped him up. "Tripped over a tail!" howled Chedd. "What a mighty hero!"

That's it! All of a sudden, Tabby knew just what to do. She took a deep breath. Then she stood up and stepped into the light of the fire.

"Tabby!" whispered Clawdia, but it was too late. The three rats stared.

"Who in the name of Parmesan are you?" asked Brie.

Tabby reached into her pocket. She took out the soft, yellow piece of cheese she had found at the royal goldsmith's shop. "Want some?" she asked.

Chedd's jaw dropped. Brie's tummy rumbled. Mozz began to drool.

"Here you go!" said Tabby. And she tossed the cheese up in the air.

The rats dived for it, snatching with their paws. First Chedd had the cheese, then Brie. They began to squawk and squabble. They fought each other to grab hold of the precious lump.

"Come on, Clawdia!" called Tabby. She rushed forward and picked up Mozz's tail. The rat was too busy reaching for the cheese to notice. Tabby quickly knotted the tip to the end of Brie's tail. *Now you can trip over your tails, too*, she thought. *See how you like it!*

Clawdia grinned and ran out from behind the rock. She took Chedd's tail and tied it to the other two.

"Go, Tabby! Go, Clawdia!" yelled Felix.

Tabby climbed onto Clawdia's shoulders and stood on her tip-paws, reaching for the peg on the wall. *Yes!* She was just tall enough to reach the key.

Finally, Brie saw what was happening. She charged, but fell over, dragging Mozz and Chedd with her. They all ended up in a hairy pile on the ground.

"Watch it, Brie!" growled Chedd.

"Has anybody seen the cheese?" asked Brie.

"I'm all tangled up!" cried Mozz.

"Serves you right for laughing at my brother!" said Tabby. She leaped to the ground, ran to the cage, and unlocked it.

Felix and Leo jumped out. Tabby and Clawdia untied their paws, and the two princes wrapped them up in a big group hug.

"Wow," said Leo, his whiskers shaking with excitement. "You two are so brave . . . just like the great Silverpaw!"

Tabby shook her head. "We were really scared!"

"But you saved us, anyway," said Felix. "That makes you even braver!"

Clawdia grinned. Then a frown passed across her face. "I just remembered . . . We still don't have the Golden Scroll! It'll be night soon. And you know what that means . . ."

"When the last sunbeam of the day falls on the Golden Scroll," said Felix, "Gorgonzola's wicked laws will come true. We can't let that happen!"

"You'll never stop him!" cackled Mozz. He tried to stand, but his tail was still tied to the others.

"Just you wait!" said Tabby. "Come on— let's get back to the palace. Mewtopia needs us!"

Chapter 8

MEDDLING KITTIES

The sun was much lower in the sky when they finally got out of the mines. Clawdia had led them out of King Gorgonzola's castle, taking every tunnel that sloped upward.

"Nearly sunset," said Felix, frowning. "We don't have much time!"

They dashed across the meadow, ran through the streets of the town, and joined the great crowd of cats flowing in through the palace gates.

Everyone was chatting excitedly. Young kittens waved flags, and almost everyone was dressed in red and gold. Felix and Leo pulled their scarves up over their noses again; Tabby kept her head down low. She pushed into the middle of the crowd so that the guards wouldn't recognize them as they passed.

A few minutes later, they were inside the Great Hall. Orange sunbeams shone through the huge window at the far end, glinting off the golden thrones on the stage.

"I didn't know there were this many cats in the whole kingdom!" said Leo. The hall was packed, kitizens talking and shuffling to get a look at the stage.

"The ceremony was supposed to start by now!" said Felix.

Tabby felt her whiskers shake with worry. "I don't like this," she said. "Mom and Dad are never late for breakfast, let alone the Golden Scroll Ceremony! Where do you think they are?"

"We could ask one of the guards," Clawdia suggested. But when the kittens looked around, there were none in sight. *They're probably all looking for Mom and Dad!* thought Tabby. Which means . . .

Has Gorgonzola gotten to them, too?

A great gasp rose from the crowd.

Tabby turned around and saw that a figure had stepped onto the stage. *Oh no!*

It was King Gorgonzola, dressed in a torn gray cloak and an iron crown. He pulled the Golden Scroll from his cloak and held it up. The crowd gasped again. The sunbeams made the gold shine and sparkle.

"Silence, kitties!" squeaked Gorgonzola. "And don't look so surprised. I am your true king, after all! Or I will be, just as soon as I've read out my new laws. I'm afraid you're not going to like them very much!"

"We have to do something!" said Leo as King Gorgonzola began to open the scroll.

All around, kitizens were panicking, looking to the sides of the hall. But the guards were still nowhere to be seen.

"It's up to us," said Tabby. *And now there's no time to be afraid!* She frowned hard, thinking. *What would Silverpaw do?* "If the last sunbeam hits that scroll, it's over," she said. "But if we could block the sunlight somehow . . ."

"What could we use?" wondered Felix.

The royal kittens looked around the hall.

"Got it!" said Leo. He pointed at the red banners hanging high up on the walls.

"Of course!" said Tabby. "Great idea, Leo."

"Um, do we have to?" asked Felix,

chewing his claws. His whiskers were shaking. "Climbing out of the tower was bad enough . . ."

"Don't worry," Tabby told him, remembering how scared she'd felt outside the mine. *It's my turn to be brave!* "You stay here, Felix. Clawdia, you look for our mom and dad. Leo, let's block that sunlight!"

The three kittens scattered. The hall was so crowded it was hard to move, but Tabby managed to dodge between legs and duck under tails. She spotted Clawdia walking toward a doorway at the side of the hall. Tabby pushed on, heading for a corner beside the stage.

At last, she reached it. *Now to get up to the banners!* Tabby slid her claws between the stones of the wall and began to climb. She glanced over her shoulder and saw Leo on the far side, climbing, too. He was half-way up the side of a banner, next to the great ceremonial window. *Go, Leo!*

The sunlight was ruby red now. As it hit the scroll, a glow began to form around King Gorgonzola. He shone with every color of sunset, and the iron crown turned golden in the magical light. Gorgonzola showed his teeth in a wicked grin.

"Quick!" yelled Tabby. "Cut down the banner!"

Leo finally reached the top of the banner. He whipped out his sword and began to saw at the rope holding it up.

"Throw it here!" Tabby cried.

Leo took the end of the rope and tossed it all the way across the Great Hall.

"Catch it, Tabby!" shouted Felix from somewhere in the crowd.

Tabby reached out with her tail. *Got it!* She wrapped the tip of her tail around the end of the rope. Then she pulled it tight, still clinging to the wall with her claws.

The banner streamed out below, covering the whole window and blocking the golden sunbeams. The Great Hall turned crimson.

We did it!

Below, cats began to cheer. King Gorgonzola spun around and glared at Tabby. His grin turned into a snarl of fury. "Meddling kitties!" he spat. "The first law is that I am the ruler of the land!"

But even as he spoke, the glow around him began to fade away. A moment later, it was gone entirely.

Gorgonzola stamped his foot and whipped his tail. "Why is nothing happening?" he screamed.

"Because it's over!" called Leo from up

high. "You're just a stinky rat, and you'll never be king of Mewtopia!"

"You'll regret saying that, little scaredy-cat!" growled Gorgonzola. He strode toward Leo.

Tabby swallowed hard. *You can do it, Tabby!* Leaping from the wall, she caught the edge of the banner with one paw and shot downward. *Rrrrriiipp!* Her claws tore four long holes, slowing her fall until she landed— *thump!*—on the stage. The banner fell away, revealing the sunset again.

Tabby drew her sword as King Gorgonzola turned to face her. His eyes looked wild with anger, and Tabby felt herself begin to shake. "Give us the scroll," she said, trying

to sound as brave as she possibly could. "Or we'll take it from you!"

Gorgonzola's claws curled... Then he threw back his head and laughed. "Ha! *You?* A pampered little pussycat? You think you're smarter than—"

Whumph!

Leo came diving down and landed on

King Gorgonzola's head. The rat fell flat, with the kitten on top of him. His crown went rolling off the stage.

"Take that!" cried Leo, grinning and bouncing up and down on the rat king's back.

Something black flashed through the crowd and shot up beside Tabby. *Felix!* He ran forward and snatched the scroll from Gorgonzola's paw. Then he tossed it to Tabby.

BANG!

Every door in the Great Hall flew open at once. Guards rushed in, all dressed in red and carrying silver swords.

"That's him!" shouted Clawdia, pointing

at Gorgonzola. She was riding on the shoulders of a guard.

Then two figures stepped through the main doors, dressed in royal robes. Tabby felt a smile spread across her face at the sight of them. *Mom! Dad!* She pulled her cloak up over her face so they wouldn't recognize her.

"Guards!" said King Pouncalot. "Arrest that rat!"

Chapter 9

THE TRUE LAWS

"You'll never catch me!" King Gorgonzola shouted. He threw Leo off and ran across the stage. *Smash!* He leaped through the great window, shattering the glass.

"After him!" ordered Queen Elizapet.

Tabby dashed to a side door and slipped through. She raced down a spiral staircase that led to the courtyard. She could hear Leo and Felix hurrying after her.

They ran out into the evening light. *There he is!* Gorgonzola was standing by a colorful display of fireworks, holding a flaming torch. He bared his yellow teeth at them. "This isn't over, kitties!" he snarled. Then he lowered the torch. *Fzzzz...* The fuses lit one by one ...

"Look out!" shouted Felix.

The royal kitties dived to the ground. Just in time, they covered their ears.

Whhoooosh! The fireworks shot up in a cloud of colorful sparks. *BANG!* A rainbow of lights floated through the evening sky.

"Whoa!" breathed Leo. "They really are amazing!"

Tabby blinked and looked around the courtyard again ... but King Gorgonzola was nowhere to be seen.

Guards came clattering out of the door behind them. "Where is he?" said one.

Tabby shook her head. "He must have slipped away."

"You look familiar," said the guard. He narrowed his eyes at the three kittens. "Do I know you?"

Uh-oh! Tabby tugged her cloak up over her face again. "Actually, we should be going."

"Wait!" called the guard. But Tabby, Leo, and Felix were already running off through the courtyard, tails waving behind them.

A few moments later, they had dashed up the back staircases to their rooms in the tower and changed into their royal clothes again. Tabby looked over at the study chamber and saw that Nanny Mittens's rocking chair was empty. *Uh-oh . . . I hope she isn't too worried about us!* But there was no time to think about that now. Tabby led the way back to the Great Hall.

The palace was still in chaos. Cats were rushing in every direction, talking anxiously to one another. Guards hunted everywhere.

"It must be here!" boomed King

Pouncalot's voice from the stage. "Where is the Golden Scroll?"

Tabby drew the scroll from her belt. She shared a glance with Felix and Leo. Then she bent down and pretended to pick it up from the floor. "Here, Dad!" she called. "That evil rat must have dropped it!"

King Pouncalot and Queen Elizapet stared wide-eyed at the royal kittens. Then

they swept off the stage, pushed through the crowd, and pulled them all into a tight hug. The Great Hall echoed with cheers and applause.

"Where have you been?" Queen Elizapet asked when she finally let go. "We were so worried . . . Nanny Mittens has been beside herself!"

The big white cat came hurrying through the crowd toward them. "Leaping fleas, there you are! Wherever have you been, my little fluffballs?"

Tabby looked up into the worried faces of her parents and Nanny Mittens.

She wasn't sure what to say. *If I tell them what really happened, they'll never let us out of the palace again! We'll never get to go exploring. Never have another adventure . . .*

"Sorry," she said at last. "We just went to the dungeon while Nanny was catnapping."

"Tabby was pretending to be Queen Gwenda the Fourth," said Leo.

"Like in the story you read us, Nanny," said Felix. "We're sorry. We must have lost track of time."

Nanny Mittens smiled and stroked Leo's ears. "Not to worry, my darlings. I'm just glad you're safe."

"Indeed," said King Pouncalot. He frowned at the kittens for a moment, then nodded. "Well, it's lucky that brave kitten Clawdia came to find us. That wicked rat locked us in our room while we were having our afternoon catnap." He frowned again. "I just wonder who her friends were . . . the ones who stopped Gorgonzola. I should like to reward them for what they've done."

"No idea, Dad," said Leo. "But I bet they know you're grateful." It was only when the king and queen turned away that he gave Tabby and Felix a wink.

"Come along, then," said Queen Elizapet. "We must read the real laws, and quickly! The last sunbeam will fade any moment now."

The royal kittens followed their parents

onto the stage. As she climbed up, Tabby spotted Clawdia in the crowd and grinned at her. Clawdia grinned back. She was standing by a grown-up cat with just the same brown-and-black pattern she had. *That must be the royal goldsmith*, Tabby thought. He was smiling proudly, his tail curled around his daughter's shoulders.

"Attention, kitizens!" said King Pouncalot. His voice echoed through the hall, and everyone went quiet at once. "We will now read the true laws of Mewtopia!"

As the king and queen opened the Golden Scroll, the sunshine sparkled and shone around them with its magical light. They began to read the laws, and every word they spoke appeared in swirling letters on the scroll.

Tabby couldn't stop smiling. They had done it. They had saved Mewtopia! She thought of King Gorgonzola, with his crooked teeth and his greasy fur. Maybe he was already planning more mischief . . . But somehow, Tabby didn't feel frightened at all.

Do your worst, rat king. The royal kittens are ready for you!

Don't miss Princess Tabby's next quest!

KITTEN KINGDOM
#2: Tabby and the Pup Prince

"Prince Hairy?" Tabby called. She crawled under the table, but she didn't see the puppies.

It's like he disappeared! Tabby was just about to give up, when she heard Captain Edmund cry out.

"It's not working!"

Tabby ran out from under the table. Captain Edmund was holding up the orb, staring at it and looking confused.

"Try it again!" said a cook.

With one paw on a big pile of dog biscuits, and the other holding the orb, Captain Edmund said:

"Orb of Plenty, hear my call.

Show your magic, feed us all!"

But there was no blue light. No magic at all. The pile of dog biscuits stayed just the same size. All around, the cooks began to whisper to one another in fear.

"I don't understand!" said Captain Edmund. He looked closely at the orb. "Something must be wrong with it. Now we will never have enough food for the feast! The dog king will think it's some kind of trick, and we will lose our chance at peace with Barkshire!"

Felix began to chew his claws again. "I don't like this," he said.

"Do you think someone broke the orb on purpose?" asked Tabby.

"But who would do that?" asked Leo.

The three kittens all spoke at the same time. "King Gorgonzola!"